Nella
and the
Dragon

By Mickie Matheis

Based on the teleplay by Kevin Del Aguila

Illustrated by Dan Haskett and Brenda Goddard-Laurence

🌹 A GOLDEN BOOK • NEW YORK

T#: 530898
ISBN 978-1-5247-1676-9
Printed in the United States of America
10 9 8 7 6 5 4 3 2 1

Princess Nella and her friends were playing in the royal sandbox. They had built a castle with sand towers, a sand drawbridge, and even a sandy moat.

"I'll add a sand hair-and-nail boutique!" said Trinket the unicorn with a toss of her mane.

Just then, the friends were interrupted by a strange sound. They looked up to see Sir Blaine stumbling their way.

"What's wrong?" Nella asked the young knight.

"A d-d-dragon . . . ," Sir Blaine stammered.

"What happened?" asked Sir Garrett. "Did it grab you? Stomp on you? Bump you with its tail?"

"Dragon . . . breathed . . . on me," he gasped. "With . . . stinky breath! PEEE-YOO!"

Nella and Sir Garrett looked toward the town square and saw people running everywhere! Soon they understood why. Smelgly, a troublesome dragon from a nearby forest, was headed right for the sandbox!

Smelgly rudely bumped Nella and Sir Garrett aside and plopped down—right on top of the sand castle! Then she grabbed Clod's bucket and started to dig.

"Hey!" Clod said.

Smelgly just laughed and kept on digging.

Suddenly, trumpets blared. Castlehaven's royal Knight Brigade was coming, ready to save the kingdom from Smelgly. The dragon blew a big puff of her stinky breath at the charging knights. They collapsed on the ground, coughing and choking.

"That wasn't nice," Nella said.

"Humph!" the crabby dragon responded, picking up the bucket and stomping back to the forest. "I can see when I'm not wanted!"

The townspeople watched her leave.

"Who's going to stop Smelgly from bothering us again?" one of them asked worriedly.

"I am," Nella said. "It's time to be a Princess Knight!" Nella's Knightly Heart necklace began to glow, transforming her into a Princess Knight. She would make things right by stopping Smelgly from scaring the kingdom.

Nella led the way into the forest to find Smelgly. Clod chomped on some leaves as they walked.

"Mmm!" he said. "These taste like mint."

"That's because they're mint leaves," Trinket explained.

Clod was amazed. "I wonder how many other flavors of leaves there are!"

Nella pointed ahead to some drooping flowers along the forest path. "Smelgly's got to be close."

Just then, they heard a giggle and stomping footsteps.

Smelgly jumped out from behind a tree. She smacked
Sir Garrett and Clod, knocking them over.
"Tag—you're it!" the dragon yelled.

As Sir Garrett and Clod got to their feet, Nella spoke firmly to Smelgly. "That wasn't nice. It wasn't nice to smash our sand castle, either."

Smelgly frowned. "Well, *fine*—be that way!" She took a deep breath and opened her mouth wide.

"Run!" Sir Garrett yelled.

Nella and her friends raced away through the forest, leaping over logs and ducking under branches. They jumped into a pond—just in time for the cloud of smelly breath to float past them.

"That was close!" Sir Garrett said. "Maybe we should leave Smelgly alone."

But Nella wasn't ready to give up. She and her friends found the dragon in a clearing.

They watched as Smelgly tried to join a game of catch with Minatori and Gork the orc. When the two creatures went off to play without her, she slumped to the ground and began to cry.

"I think she just wants a friend," Nella said.
She began to walk over to Smelgly, and the
dragon stood up, readying her stinky breath.

"Smelgly—wait," Nella said. "If you're looking for a friend, maybe I can help."

The dragon looked very sad. "Nobody will play with me because of my stinky breath."

"It might not be your breath. It might be the way you act sometimes," Nella said kindly. "If you really want to make friends, don't snarl or growl. Smile at others and show them you're friendly."

Sir Garrett chimed in. "And give them space. Don't bump into them or get right in their faces."

"And share your toys!" Trinket and Clod added.

Nella nodded. "Yes! That way everyone has something to play with."

Smelgly looked thoughtful. Making friends didn't sound that hard! She couldn't wait to try. But she was still nervous about something. "What about . . . my breath?"

"Don't worry," Nella said. "I've got a plan."

They took Smelgly back to the pond. Nella tossed her sword into the air and it transformed into a lance. Garrett tied a bunch of mint leaves to the end of it to make a giant toothbrush.

Then Nella used it to brush Smelgly's teeth! Clod brought a bucket of water to rinse Smelgly's mouth.

Next, Nella transformed the lance into a bow and arrow. She tied one end of a ribbon to the arrow and shot it to Trinket. Clod grabbed the ribbon, and together they flossed Smelgly's teeth.

The dragon smiled at her reflection in the pond. Her teeth sparkled!

The friends returned to the kingdom with Smelgly. The dragon blew a fresh, minty breeze across the town square. "Mmmm!" the townspeople said, sniffing the air.

Smelgly headed straight for the royal sandbox, where Princess Norma was playing. "Can I play, too?" Smelgly asked.

"Mmm-hmm!" Princess Norma said.

Smelgly sat at the other end of the sandbox so the princess had plenty of room.

"Will you share your shovel?" the dragon asked politely, holding out the bucket.

The two happily traded toys.

The townspeople looked at one another. Smelgly was behaving so nicely!

Nella, Sir Garrett, Trinket, and Clod climbed into the sandbox, too. Everyone worked together to build a new sand castle.

The dragon was having so much fun. "Thanks for everything, guys!" she said.

"Of course, Smelgly!" Nella said. "But I forgot to tell you one thing."

"What?" the dragon asked.

"Tag! You're it!" Nella said.

And the happy dragon ran off with her new friends.